Gabriella Garbage Truck

Dump Truck Dan

Hook and Ladder Lucy

Pumper Pat

Rescue Rita

Payloader Pete

Cement Mixer Melvin

Big Rig

Grader Kat

Jack Truck

Monster Truck Max

Izzy Ice Cream Truck

Tow Truck Ted

SIMON AND SCHUSTER
First published in Great Britain in 2008 by
Simon and Schuster UK Ltd
Africa House, 64-78 Kingsway, London WC2B 6AH
A CBS company

Originally published in 2008 by
Simon and Schuster Books for Young Readers,
an imprint of Simon & Schuster
Children's Publishing Division, New York

Book design by Dan Potash
A CIP catalogue record for this book is available
from the British Library

ISBN: 978 1 84738 274 0
Printed in China
10 9 8 7 6 5 4 3 2 1

Characters and environments
developed by the

DESIGN
garage

David Shannon • Loren Long • David Gordon

To my pre-K Trucktown pals:
Allie, Angela, Ayinde, Bea, Caleb, Caitlin, Camilla,
Danny, Gregory, Henry, Jasmine, Laura, Lukas,
Malcolm, Martin, Mira, William, Yosef, Amileon, Claire,
Conor, Eli, Gabriela, Gerard, Iman, Julian, Kade,
Kennedy, Laura, Maxine, Michael, Mollie, Roman, Ryan,
Ruby, Sofia, and their wonderful teachers Marie and
Rose, Idalis and Jenny, Meriss and Aida.
– JS

ILLUSTRATION CREW

Executive producer

Keytoon INC.

in association with
ANIMAGIC S.L.

Creative Supervisor
Sergio Pablos

Drawings by
Juan Pablo Navas

Colour by
Isabel Nadal

Art director
Dan Potash

SMASH! CRASH!

written by
Jon Scieszka

Jon Scieszka's TRUCKTOWN

SIMON AND SCHUSTER
London   New York   Sydney

Jack Truck.

Dump Truck Dan.

Best friends.

Jack and Dan.

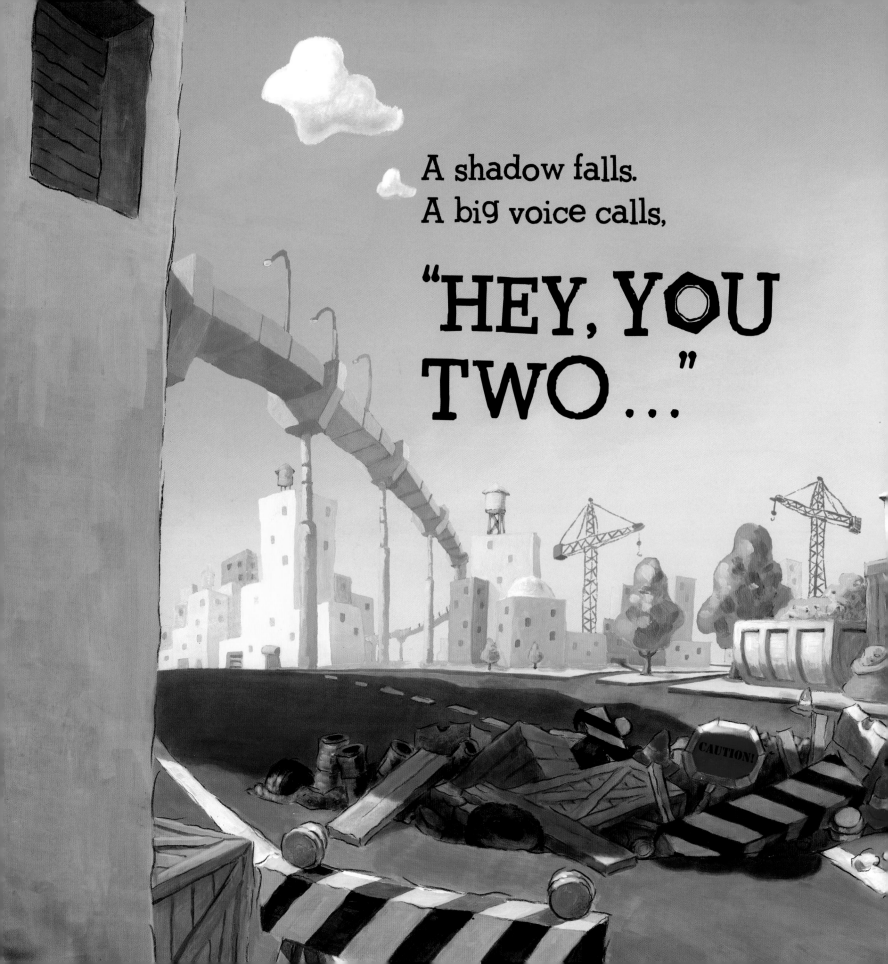

A shadow falls.
A big voice calls,

"HEY, YOU
TWO..."

Jack and Dan hit the road.
"Uh-oh."
"Got to go!"

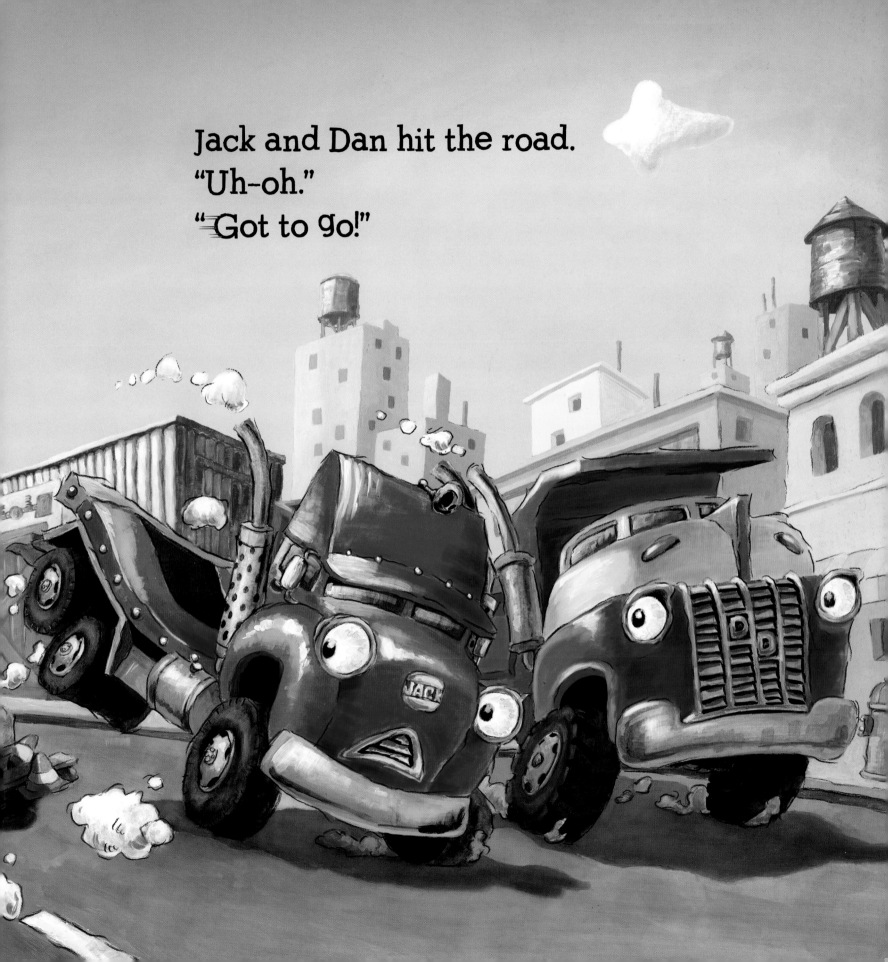

Jack and Dan zoom up to Cement Mixer Melvin.

"Melvin!" calls Jack. "Time to smash!"
"Melvin!" yells Dan. "Time to crash!"

But Melvin is busy.
"No, I can't get messy.
I'm mixing,
mixing, mixing."

Jack winks at Dan and they ...

"You mixed it all," says Melvin.
"You also made a mess."

A clank. A rumble.
It must mean trouble.

"HEY, YOU TWO.
I WANT YOU."

Jack and Dan step on the gas.
"Uh-oh."
"Got to go."

Jack and Dan roll up to Monster Truck Max.
"Hey, Max," says Jack. "Help us smashing!"
"Yeah, Max," says Dan. "Help us crashing!"

But Max is awfully busy.

Suddenly there's a
weird voice calling.
"Oh, no," says Jack. "It's – "

"Do you want an ice cream?"

"Do you want an ice cream?"

"Do you want an ice cream?"

"It's Izzy!" says Dan.
"Not now, Izzy," says Jack.
Jack and Dan speed away.

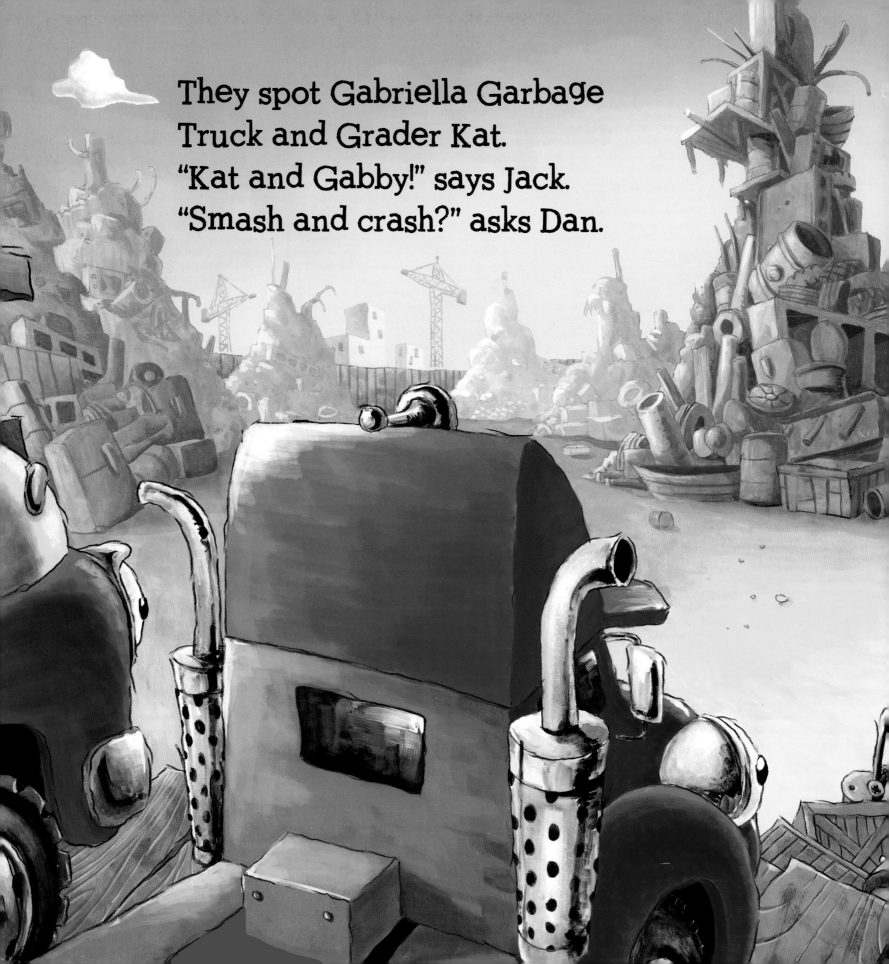

They spot Gabriella Garbage
Truck and Grader Kat.
"Kat and Gabby!" says Jack.
"Smash and crash?" asks Dan.

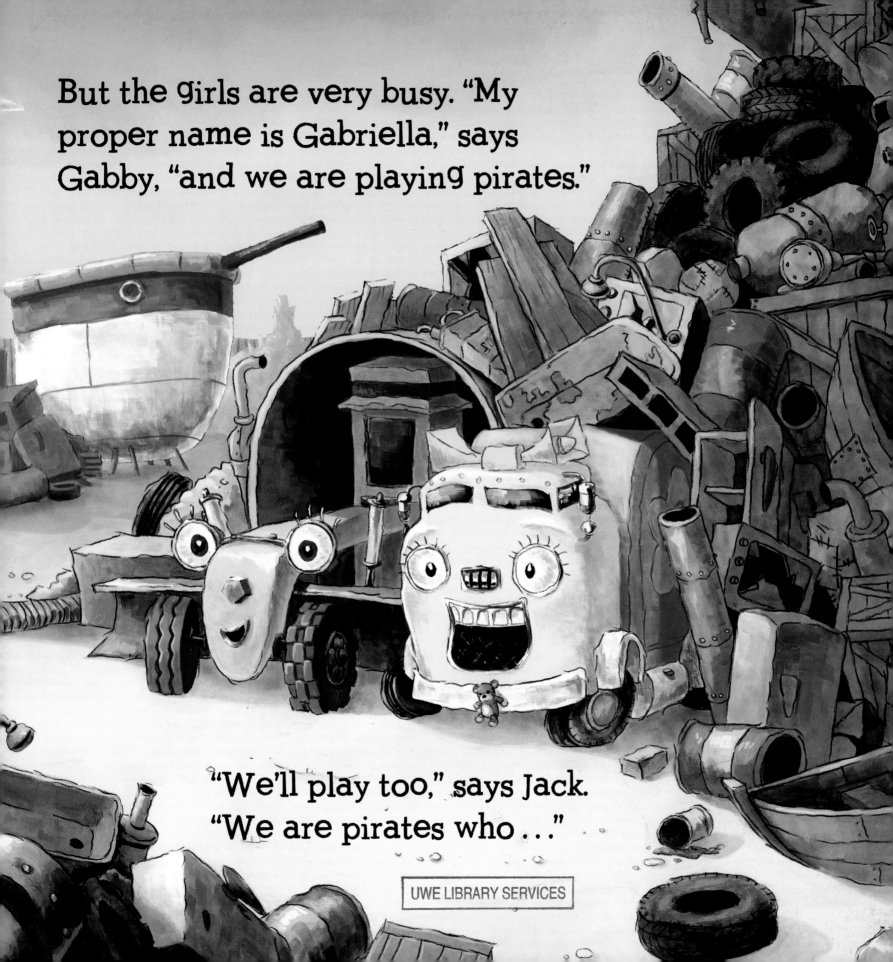

But the girls are very busy. "My proper name is Gabriella," says Gabby, "and we are playing pirates."

"We'll play too," says Jack. "We are pirates who . . ."

SMASH.

CRASH!

SMASH.

CRASH!

"A perfect pirate ship!" says Kat.

"Fabulous!" says Gabby.

That shadow grows LARGER.
That voice calls LOUDER.

"HEY, YOU TWO.
I WANT
YOU.

I WANT
YOU TO . . ."

Jack and Dan try to
race away, but . . .
"Oh, no!"
"No go!"

It's Wrecking Crane Rosie.
Rosie is huge.
Rosie is strong.
Rosie booms,
"FOLLOW ME."

"HEY YOU TWO. I WANT YOU. I WANT YOU TO..."

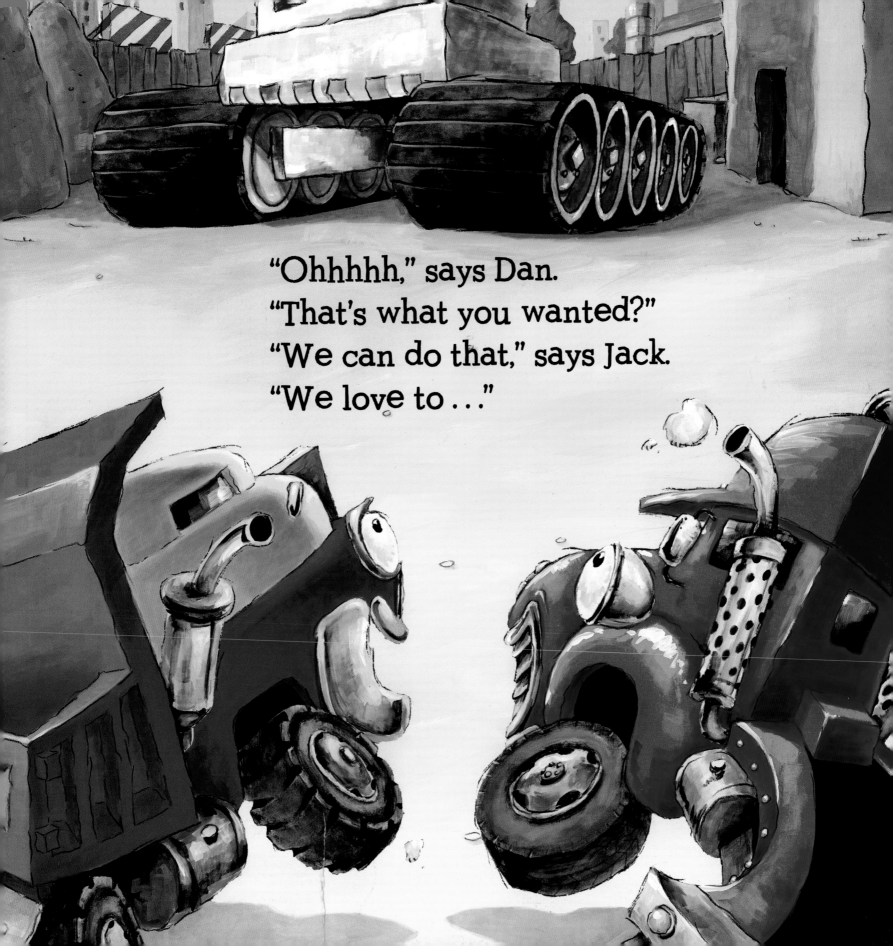

"Let me tell you something."

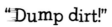

"Dump dirt!"

"Me too!?"

"Heh, heh, heh."

"Follow me!"

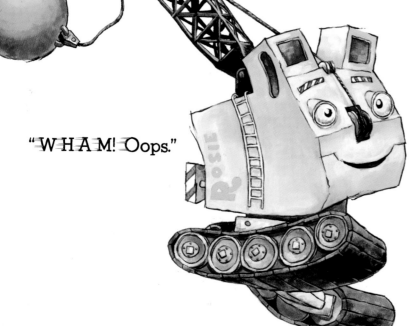

"WHAM! Oops."

"I don't want to."

"Out of my way."

"Quiet, please. I'm dreaming!"

"To the MAX!"

"Rules are ...

... rules."

"Do you want an ice cream?
Do you want an ice cream?
Do you want an ice cream?"

"I have a plan."